THE LION *and the* MOUSE

For Lambkin, who is herself a lion of sorts

A TEMPLAR BOOK

Published in the United States in 1995 by The Millbrook Press, Inc.
2 Old New Milford Road, Brookfield, CT 06804

Devised and produced by The Templar Company plc
Pippbrook Mill, London Road, Dorking, Surrey RH4 1JE, Great Britain

Illustrations copyright © 1995 by Ian Andrew
This edition copyright © 1995 by The Templar Company plc

Designed by Mike Jolley

Library of Congress Cataloguing-in-Publication Data

Wood. A. J., 1960–
The lion and the mouse : an Aesop's fable / retold by A.J. Wood :
illustrated by Ian Andrews.
p.   cm.
Summary: A tiny mouse helps a mighty lion, who once showed him mercy, escape from a trap.
ISBN 1-56294-658-7 (LIB. BDG.) 1-56294-933-0 (TR.)
[1. Fables.] I. Aesop. II. Andrews, Ian P., 1962– ill.
III. Title.
PZ8.2.W7L1   1995
398.2 — dc20   — dc20
[E]
[398.24'52974428]   95–19193
CIP
AC

Printed in Italy

an Aesop's fable

THE LION and the MOUSE

Retold by **A.J. WOOD** *Illustrated by* **IAN ANDREW**

THE MILLBROOK PRESS
Brookfield, Connecticut

All through the long afternoon, the forest slept.

Beneath the burning sun nothing moved nor made a sound.

Nothing, but the cry of the dark and hungry birds

that circled endlessly overhead.

Nothing, but the butterflies

that sometimes danced

in the trees' cool shade.

Suddenly, a new sound broke the silence.

It was a lion.

He lifted his golden head and roared.

He roared his majesty to the trees and

the birds and the fluttering butterflies.

"Look at me!" his roar seemed to say.

"*I am King.* Let no creature come before me."

And then, satisfied that he had made his presence felt,

the lion continued on his way.

Above, amongst the branches, his startled subjects watched him go.

Below, another creature hid, trapped within the leafy carpet of the lion's path.

It was a mouse.

He stayed, still as stone,

his tiny heart beating with the memory of the lion's roar.

He crouched, silent as rock, until the shadow of the lion's

paw had passed.

And then the mouse, too,

continued on his way.

Hours passed.

In the quiet of the forest, Lion yawned and lay down to sleep. He dreamed of

soothing rain and silver rivers, and of the endless water that was the sea.

But he awoke to the pitter-patter

not of raindrops but of something

else, to a rustling just beneath his

nose and the slightest touch on

the fur of his great velvet paw.

Lion opened his shining sleepy yellow eyes and looked.

There before him crouched a mouse.

"Forgive me, Lord Lion," squeaked the tiny creature.

"I did not see you sleeping there. To me, your paw

was a hill of golden sand. Let me go and I will

disturb you no more."

And Mouse waited for Lion to speak, certain that only death could now await him.

"And why should *I* forgive *you*?" snarled Lion, licking his lips.

"What reason could I possibly have?"

Mouse thought awhile and then replied: "Because one day

I may be able to spare your life in return."

Lion smiled a slow, sleepy smile, for he thought Mouse's story most unlikely.

But there was kindness deep in the lion's heart. So he growled, "Be off with you,"

and watched as Mouse scampered away.

And the mouse looked back at the lion who had spared him and wondered...

Lion slept on until evening came to the forest.

Deep in his dreams, he did not hear

the sound of footsteps in the shadows

until it was too late.

Too late.

He woke again just as the golden net fell.

And Lion found himself bound fast,

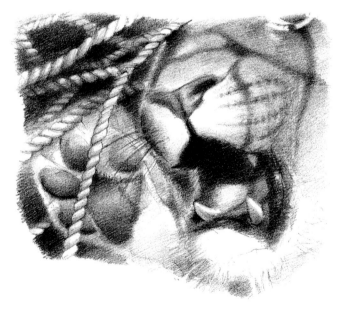

trapped into a still waiting

while his captors left

to fetch their knives.

No one could help Lion now, or so he thought.

But nearby someone was watching,

someone who remembered his kindness.

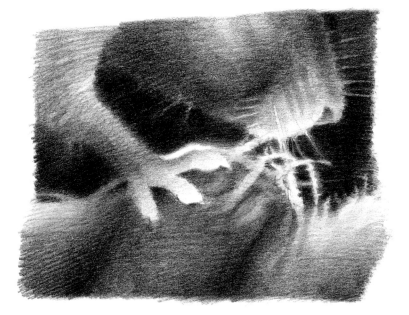

And if you had been listening then to the sounds of the forest,

you may have heard another noise among the buzzing and the

birdcalls and the rustling of a thousand leaves.

For Mouse was busy gnawing, gnawing with his sharp, white,

pointed teeth, gnawing until the strands of golden rope fell away

and Lion was *free*.

"You were right to spare me after all," said Mouse, as Lion stepped forth

once again into the darkness of the forest.

And the great Lord Lion looked at the mouse as if for the first

time, two great, golden eyes peering into two quick, brown ones.

Then he bowed his head in the

knowledge of a lesson learned

and both went on their way.

The Moral

It holds through the whole scale of Creation,

that the Great and the Little have need, one of another.